WHAT COLOR IS CAESAR?

McGraw-Hill Book Company   New York   St. Louis   San Francisco

WHAT COLOR IS CAESAR?

by Maxine Kumin

illustrated by Evaline Ness

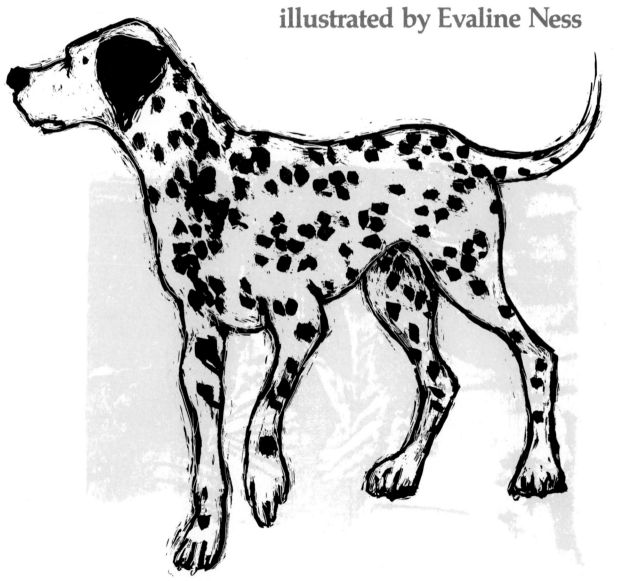

Library of Congress Cataloging in Publication Data

Kumin, Maxine W   What color is Caesar?

SUMMARY: Caesar doesn't know if he is a white dog
with black spots or a black dog with white spots.
[1. Dogs—Fiction]   I. Ness, Evaline.   II. Title.
PZ7.K949017Wf   [e]   77-17474   ISBN 0-07-035638-6

To Arnold Bayard (E.N.)

A LARGE DOG named Caesar, which is a name of kings and emperors, was very worried about the way he looked. Caesar was either all white with a great many black spots or all black with even more white ones. And that was the trouble. He didn't know which.

Nobody in the family could tell him. But nobody seemed to care. They patted him on the head. They tickled him on the stomach. They said, *Good dog!* and *Sit!* and *Stay!* and sometimes they said, *Come!* They fed him lovely dinners out of his own dish and even the baby, who was only two years old, never pulled his tail, although she wanted to. "No, no," she said out loud to herself. It was her favorite word that year.

■ "Black spots or white spots, what difference does it make?" asked Petunia the cat, who was only named after a flower. She was all black with four white feet and a white nose. "Take me, for instance. I'm black and white but I never give it a moment's thought. It's quite enough to know I'm a cat." She smiled a superior smile. And she started washing her face all over again, although it was perfectly clean to begin with.

"I don't know what difference it makes," said Caesar. "But it does. Maybe I'm just run down and that's why I worry about my spots. I think I'll go to the doctor for a checkup."

The doctor, who happened to be a black and white woodpecker with a bright red dot on the top of his head, looked Caesar over. He listened to his heart and peeked in his ears and tested his legs with a little rubber hammer.

"Hmm," he said. "Your ears are dirty and your toenails are much too long. But your nose is cold and all four of your legs work. I think you are in perfectly good shape for a spotted dog. Let me see you wag your tail."

Caesar wagged.

"Now open your mouth and say ahh."

Caesar said ahh for a long time while the woodpecker peered down his throat.

"Just as I thought," he said. "Inside you are gray with pink spots! Or is it pink with gray spots?"

Caesar stopped saying *ahh* so fast that the woodpecker barely had time to get his head out safely. "What does it mean?"

"Basically?"

"Basically," Caesar repeated. He did not know exactly what the word meant, but now he was more worried than ever.

■ "It means you are either all white with a great many black spots or all black with a great many more white ones. That is, on the outside. Inside, as you know, it's a matter of pink and gray or gray and pink, depending on how you look at it."

"But basically," Caesar asked, "which would you say?"

"I really wouldn't want to make a guess," replied the woodpecker. "Take me, for instance. On the outside I appear to be black and white, don't I?"

Caesar nodded.

"But basically, of course, I am bright red. You can see that, can't you?"

Caesar didn't know whether to answer yes or no, so he shook his head and wagged his tail at the same time.

"Of course I'm red," said the woodpecker. "Basically. And you really should brush your teeth more often. That will be ten dollars, please."

Caesar paid the woodpecker and sadly went back home. He tried to forget his troubles by chasing Petunia around the living room. Then he played on the floor with the baby. But even while he was fetching the ball and bringing it back to her, he went on brooding. Which am I, he wondered. Basically white or basically black? Will I ever find out?

Early the next day Caesar left home to seek the answer. He had only gone a little way when he met a large black and white cow who was lying under a tree in a pasture.

"Pardon me, Madame," he said timidly. "Have you noticed that we look alike?"

The cow swished her tail. "Alike?" she said, puzzled. "What is your daily average milk production? Let me hear you moo."

"Of course I am merely a dog," Caesar said modestly. "And you are a cow. But have you noticed that we are, ah, the same colors?"

"Now that you mention it. Purple and blue, right?"

"No, I don't think so. I think we are black and white."

"Is that so?" said the cow, interested. "I never studied colors before. So that's what black and white are." And she turned to examine the black and white splotches on her sides. "Which one is which?"

Caesar showed her. "Now perhaps you can tell me," he asked, "are you all black with white spots or all white with black spots? I mean, basically."

"Basically," replied the cow, chewing her cud so that her jaws moved from side to side like a typewriter, "basically and deep down I am the color of milk. Which I believe is called pink."

"Pink milk? No, I don't think so. The color of milk is…is cream color. Cream color is yellowish white, or whitish yellow. Milk color. Milk is the color of milk."

"Well, that's what I am," the cow said firmly. "I told you so in the first place. Now if you don't mind, I have work to do. I have this whole meadow of grass to eat before the sun goes down."

Caesar thanked the cow politely and went on his way. He was more confused than ever. In the next field he saw a handsome black and white pony cantering along the fence.

"Hello there, rabbit," said the pony. "How are things?"

"I beg your pardon, but you made a little mistake," Caesar answered. "I am a dog. And things aren't too good right now."

"Terribly sorry," said the pony. "The truth is, I haven't met many dogs before this. I was running so fast that I mistook you for a rabbit. What seems to be the trouble?"

"Well," Caesar began. "You may have noticed that you and I are more or less the same colors. Black and white, that is."

The pony danced around, craning his neck to get a good look at himself.

"You're right! You're exactly right! Everybody always says I'm so pretty. Now I see why!"

"Well, here is my problem," Caesar said. "I can't decide whether we are all white with a great many black spots or all black with even more white spots. Basically, that is."

"Oh, what an easy question!" The pony raced around in a wide circle snorting and bucking. "Ask me something hard! Ask me about walk, trot, and canter. Ask me about standing still or backing up. Ask me how to eat a sugar lump without slurping."

"I'd really rather ask you about black and white. Basically, which do you think you are?"

■ The pony stood on his hind legs for an instant and pawed the air. "Neither!"

"Neither? You *have* to be one or the other."

"Basically," said the pony, "I am pure green. That's what I am. Of course I have no way of knowing what *you* are."

"Green? How can you be green?"

"Well, it's this way, dog. I live in an all green world. I was born in this green pasture in the green month of May. I eat green timothy and green clover, and I drink green water from that old bathtub."

Caesar looked. The water was indeed green from grass juice.

"I roll in green weeds when my back itches." He did so. "I lie under a green tree when it is too hot to canter. And even the oats in my bucket, you may have noticed, are as green as a weeping willow leaf."

"Well, brownish-green," Caesar said doubtfully.

"That's what I told you," said the pony. "Green through and through. Aren't I pretty? Now if you'll excuse me, I have work to do. I must practice my prancing. That's the first thing pretty ponies have to learn if they want to join the circus."

"Circus?"

"There's a circus in the next town," the pony said. "With music and tents and lots of people to clap their hands. That's where I'm going as soon as I am old enough."

"Well, good luck," said Caesar. "And good-bye."

"Good-bye yourself," said the pony.

Caesar set out again down the road. He had never been so far from home before. As he trotted over the top of the next hill, a little town appeared in the distance. Soon he could make out the shapes of tents with flags flying from their ridgepoles. The sound of music drifted toward him as he drew nearer. All sizes and shapes of people were milling about strange animals in huge cages. One animal looked rather like a horse, but its skin was covered with bright zigzags of black and white.

"Take a good look," said the zebra, for that's what it was. "Never seen anything like me before, have you? That's because I am so special. I've come all the way from Africa for people to look at me and go ooh and ahh!"

"Yes, you are very special," said Caesar. "And I've never seen a zebra before. I don't mean to be rude about it, but have you noticed that we are a tiny, little bit alike?"

"Ridiculous!" the zebra exclaimed. "You're nothing but a dog."

"I know I'm only a dog, but what I meant was…what I meant was that we're the same colors. You may possibly have seen the resemblance. Black and white, that is."

"Black and white? You mean those funny runny spots you have all over you? They may be the same colors as my zigzags, but really, dog! The resemblance ends right there."

"Oh, I agree with you," Caesar said hurriedly. "We're very different. But could you just tell me one thing? Are you basically all white with black zigzags? Basically?"

"That's a typical dog question," said the zebra crossly. "Can't you see that basically, at heart, under the skin, I am clear yellow?"

"Yellow?"

"Stop repeating everything I say! Look into my eyes. What do you see?"

"I see yellowish-brown eyes," Caesar said. "Very handsome eyes," he added.

"Of course they're yellow," the zebra went on. "Yellow as the sun of Africa, the good bright sun that shines down on the forests and plains of my native land."

"I see," said Caesar, to be polite.

■ "You don't see, of course." The zebra shivered a little. "Nobody does. You've never galloped over the hills and through the valleys under a round hot African sun."

"To tell you the truth," said Caesar, "I haven't. I can't imagine what it's like to be basically yellow under your black and white zigzags. But that's because I've been trying for a long time to find out what color I am, basically. And I don't even know that."

The zebra seemed not to be paying attention. He munched hay in a corner of his cage. "Dreadfully dry stuff," he murmured. "The guru would know."

"The guru would know what?"

"Don't be a dumb dog. The guru would know what color you are, basically."

"But I don't even know what a guru is," Caesar said sadly.

"A guru is a wise man of the East," said the zebra. "My animal trainer, whose real name is Harry, is the fortune-telling guru of this circus. Of course he's only a make-believe guru, but that's better than no guru at all."

"Yes, I guess it is. Do you really think he can help me? Where will I find him?"

"Turn left at the end of this row of cages. Look for a little blue tent. Inside is a man who gazes deep into a crystal ball and tells people their fortunes. That's Harry."

Caesar did just as the zebra told him. He raced down the row of cages, turned left at the end and ran breathlessly to the flap of the little blue tent. Inside sat a little wrinkled gnome of a man wrapped in an enormous white sheet. On his head he wore a white turban. His feet were bare. He was sucking an orange lollipop.

"Come to have your fortune told, have you?" asked the guru hiding the lollipop under his sheet. "Well, now, let's see your ticket first."

"Oh, but I don't have any ticket," Caesar said. "I didn't exactly come to have my fortune told."

"Out of work, then, are you? Sorry, sonny. We're not hiring any more trick dogs."

"No. It isn't exactly that, either."

"Well then, speak up, sonny. We haven't got all day."

"The zebra sent me, sir," said Caesar. "My name is Caesar. I have a problem and he thought you could help me."

"Yes. Go on," said the guru more kindly.

"I have a problem about the way I look."

"Don't like your spots, eh? It's like that, is it?"

"I like them well enough. For a spotted dog, that is. But…"

"But?"

"But the thing that worries me is, what am I basically? I mean, am I basically white with black spots or black with even more white spots?"

"Hmm," said the guru. "Basically, eh?"

"Yes."

"First let me ask you what color you think I am, basically," said the guru. He took out the lollipop and had a long lick.

"I can't even guess," said Caesar. "Nobody turns out to be the color, basically, I think they are."

"For instance?"

"For instance, the cat doesn't care, the woodpecker is red, the cow is milk color, the pony is green, and the zebra is yellow."

"And?" asked the guru.

"And every one of them is just as black and white as I am. On the surface, at least."

"Exactly," said the guru.

"Yes, but exactly what?"

"You said it yourself. You are all black and white on the surface. What did you say your name was?"

"Caesar."

"Well, Caesar, it's this way. On the surface you are the color your are, and basically, under the skin, deep down, at heart, you are..."

"You are?" asked Caesar, getting excited.

The guru licked his lollipop again. "You are whatever color you want to be."

"Are you sure?"

"Of course I'm sure. I'm a guru, aren't I?"

"You're a make-believe guru," Caesar said. "That's what the zebra told me."

"Shh!" said the guru, looking around hurriedly. "Here, have a lollipop. It's true, I am only a make-believe guru, but that's better than no guru at all, isn't it?"

"I guess so," said Caesar. He chose a lollipop from the bunch the guru held out and started licking it.

"Of course these aren't very good for your teeth," warned the guru.

"No, I suppose not."

"Still, they are tasty. And they come in all colors."

"Speaking of colors," Caesar said, "what color *are* you, basically?"

"Basically, I am the color of water. Of air with no blue sky behind it. Of brand-new minnows. Of see-through plastic."

"I see," said Caesar.

"Yes," said the guru. "I am a see-through guru. Colorless. Transparent. I like it."

"It suits you," Caesar said slowly.

"Now, Caesar, let us put an end to your wandering. Let us find out what color suits *you*, basically. Close your eyes."

Caesar did so.

"Squeeze them very tight indeed," said the guru.

Caesar squeezed them so tight that his nose wrinkled.

"Empty your mind of all thoughts. No dog bones. No cat named Petunia. No baby on the floor to play ball with."

"How did you know?" Caesar asked, astonished.

"I am not a guru for nothing. Quick! Empty your mind!"

"I'm trying."

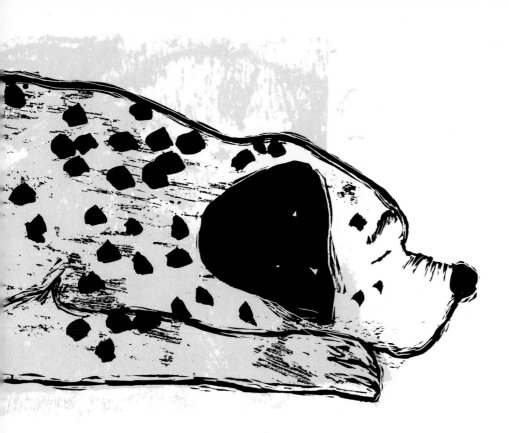

"Now tell me: what is your favorite color? Don't stop to think! Just say it."

Caesar was silent.

"Oh, come now," said the guru impatiently. "You have to help, you know. I can't do it all myself. Remember, I am only a make-believe guru."

"The trouble is," said Caesar, "what I see are all these different colors, all going around and around in bright little boxes."

"Like what?"

"Oh, red and orange and yellow and green and blue and violet and purple. Colors like that."

"Like that, eh?" asked the guru. "Do you know what that's called?"

"No, what?"

"That," said the guru, "is called a rainbow. And that's what you are, Caesar. Basically."

"A rainbow?" Caesar opened his eyes, impressed.

"Basically, you are a rainbow of colors. Just like my lollipop collection."

"Not black and white?"

"Only on the surface. Underneath you are seven colors, the seven colors of the rainbow."

Caesar closed his eyes again, tight. He wrinkled his nose so hard that he sneezed. "Why, so I am!" he said. "Now I can see it! Rainbow!"

■ Suddenly Caesar was very tired and very happy. He was hungry, too. He was a black and white spotted dog who missed his family. The rainbow colors were safe inside his head.

"Thank you," he said to the guru. "Thank you for helping me to find out what color I am, basically."

"Don't mention it," the guru replied. He licked his lollipop and looked again into his crystal ball. "From what I see here, if you hurry up, you might get home in time for dinner."

"I'll run all the way," Caesar promised.

"It looks like beef stew with lots of leftovers."

"Here I go," said Caesar. "A rainbow dog is very fast."

And he was.

About the Author

Maxine Kumin, a Pulitzer Prize-winning poet, is the author of more than twenty children's books as well. For McGraw-Hill with co-author Anne Sexton, Ms. Kumin has written THE WIZARD'S TEARS and JOEY AND THE BIRTHDAY PRESENT. She lives in Warner, New Hampshire.

About the Artist

A distinguished author in her own right, *Evaline Ness* has illustrated many outstanding books for young people, including THE WIZARD'S TEARS. Ms. Ness grew up in Pontiac, Michigan, and attended art schools in Chicago, Washington, D.C., New York, and Italy. Ms. Ness has been the recipient of the Caldecott medal for SAM, BANGS & MOONSHINE, in addition to having three Caldecott runners-up to her credit. She lives in New York City.

016676

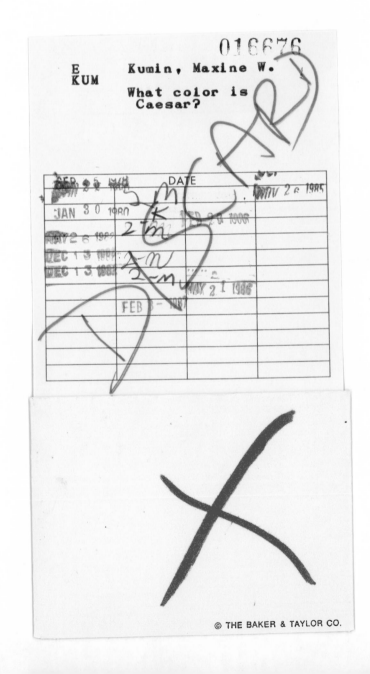

016676

E
KUM

Kumin, Maxine W.

What color is
Caesar?

	DATE		
SEP 2 5 1979			NOV 2 6 1985
JAN 3 0 1980		FEB 2 0 1986	
MAY 2 6 1982			
DEC 1 3 1982			
DEC 1 3 1982			
		MAY 2 1 1986	
	FEB 3 1987		